P9-CKC-933

InterRupting COW

New Tricks for the Old Dog

For Peter Tacy
and in memory of his old dog Gracie
who inspired this book —J. Y.

To my friend, Emilie Chazerand,
Queen of Jokes —J. D.

SIMON SPOTLIGHT
An imprint of Simon & Schuster Children's Publishing Division
1230 Avenue of the Americas, New York, New York 10020
This Simon Spotlight edition December 2021
Text copyright © 2021 by Jane Yolen
Illustrations copyright © 2021 by Joëlle Dreidemy
All rights reserved, including the right of reproduction in whole or in part in any form.
SIMON SPOTLIGHT, READY-TO-READ, and colophon are registered trademarks of
Simon & Schuster, Inc.
For information about special discounts for bulk purchases, please contact Simon & Schuster
Special Sales at 1-866-506-1949 or business@simonandschuster.com.
Manufactured in the United States of America 1121 LAK
10 9 8 7 6 5 4 3 2 1
Library of Congress Cataloging-in-Publication Data
Names: Yolen, Jane, author. I Dreidemy, Joelle, illustrator.
Title: New tricks for the Old Dog / by Jane Yolen; illustrated by Joelle Dreidemy.
Description: Simon Spotlight edition. I New York: Simon Spotlight, 2021.
Series: Interrupting Cow I Audience: Ages 5–7.
Summary: When Interrupting Cow tries to help Old Dog learn a new trick, they both end up
learning something new.
Identifiers: LCCN 2021025860 (print) I LCCN 2021025861 (ebook) I ISBN 9781534499508
(hardcover) I ISBN 9781534499492 (paperback) I ISBN 9781534499515 (ebook)
Subjects: CYAC: Cows—Fiction. I Dogs—Fiction. I Jokes—Fiction. I Humorous stories. I LCGFT:
Picture books.
Classification: LCC PZ7.Y78 Nh 2020 (print) I LCC PZ7.Y78 (ebook) I DDC [E]—dc23
LC record available at https://lccn.loc.gov/2021025860

Yolen, Jane,
New tricks for the old dog /
2021.
33305249846142
ca   12/29/21

INTERRUPTING COW

New Tricks for the Old Dog

by Jane Yolen
illustrated by Joëlle Dreidemy

Ready-to-Read

Simon Spotlight

New York   London   Toronto   Sydney   New Delhi

It was a summer morning,
which meant the light
came early into the cow barn.
The herd was enjoying their hay
and a bit of gossip.
Interrupting Cow turned
to her mates with a smile.

"Knock, knock," she said.
"Who's there?" they asked.
They never learned.
"Interrupting Cow," she said.
"Interrupting Cow w—" began
the herd.

Moo!

"MOO!" shouted Interrupting Cow. As always, she fell to the barn floor in hopeless wiggles and giggles.

But along with the light,
something else
had entered the barn.
It was an old dog.
A very old dog.

His brown coat
had turned gray.
He sniffed a lot.
And now he was giggling.
"Interrupting indeed," he said.

All the cows,
except Interrupting Cow,
fell into a tizzy,
which is a kind of cow snit.
They sniffed at the dog.

"Not funny!
Never trust a dog!"
they complained
and galloped out of the barn.

"Gosh," said Interrupting Cow,
 turning to the dog.
"You laughed at my joke.
That doesn't often happen."
"Well," he said, "it was *my* joke first.
You know: 'Knock, knock.'"
"Who's there?" asked Interrupting Cow.

The old dog smiled.
"Interrupting Dog," he said.

"But . . . but . . . but . . .
that's not how it goes,"
Interrupting Cow complained.

"Just go with the flow,"
the old dog told her,
wiggling his gray nose
until it was tied into a knot,
which was funny all by itself.

"Okay," she said,
though she was not quite sure.
"Interrupting
Dog wh—?"

"WOOF!" he barked, interrupting her, and then he fell over
in helpless wuffs and guffaws.

Interrupting Cow shook her head. "That's not funny."

"It is if you are a dog," he said,
getting up from the floor.
"An *old* dog.
It's my *best* trick."

"Then time to learn a new one,"
said Interrupting Cow.
"Even I have managed to do that,
and I am no spring chicken,
though it was a rooster
crossing a road
who taught me to try
some new material."

"But what if I am too old
to learn new tricks?"
the gray dog asked
and woofed sadly,
"Knock, knock. . . ."

But Interrupting Cow
did not ask the question.
Instead she said simply,
"Nobody is *that* old."

They went outside into the yard,
then came to the duck pond
where the ducks, who had heard
Interrupting Cow's joke
too often and never laughed,
swam quickly to the other side,
leaving a barrier of foam behind.

Interrupting Cow found a stick
on the ground and flung it
into the water, where it swam
in the ducks' wake.
"Fetch!" she called to the old dog.

The dog paddled to the stick
and brought it back.
"Another old trick," he said.

"And only a little
funny," she added.
But she smiled.
"Let me give it a
deep cow think."

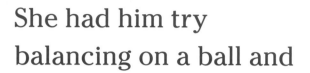

She had him try
balancing on a ball and

walking a tightrope
stretched on the ground.
It made her laugh a little more.

She had him try jumping
through a hoop.

Skipping back and forth.
Dancing the tango.
Even singing.
They began
to laugh
together.

But suddenly, the old dog slumped
on the ground.
By now he was out of breath,
out of control, and—he thought—
maybe even out of time.
"Done," he said. "I'm done.

"But we *have* found your
new trick," Interrupting Cow said.
She grinned.
"Not ball-balancing,
tightrope-walking, hoop-jumping,
skipping, dancing, or singing,
though I am glad you tried
new things."
He sighed. "You're right.
I am terrible at all of them."

Interrupting Cow smiled.
"Not so terrible, but there is
one trick that's your best.
You are great at being a friend.
That's a good new trick at any age."
He looked up and slowly grinned.
"And *you* are a great friend too,
MOO—"
"WOOF," she interrupted,
and they fell down together
in helpless laughter.